# The Adventure of the Little Long Dog

Written by Jennifer Harrison

Illustratred by Harjoyt Johal

Tellwell Talent
www.tellwell.ca

ISBN
978-0-2288-4486-0 (Paperback)
978-0-2288-4487-7 (eBook)

# Dedication

Jennifer: To the people who encouraged me to share this story with others and Baxter – thank you for choosing me to be your human.

Harjoyt: To the special people in my life who encouraged me to share my creativity with the world.

There once was a little long dog named Baxter. He lived in the Great White North with his special human. For a little long dog, Baxter had a big voice. When he had something to say, he would let his human know with a **BARK, BARK, BARK**.

When the air grew cold and the days grew short, the little long dog would sit in his special spot and watch the snowflakes fall. He loved to run through the soft powder and feel it underneath his paws. He would **BARK, BARK, BARK** to let his human know it was time to play.

When the snow melted and the days grew long, the little long dog would watch the grass grow from his special spot. He loved to chase his ball in the tall grass and smell all the smells after a long winter. He would **BARK, BARK, BARK** to let his human know it was time to play.

In the spring, the little long dog noticed that his human did not want to play when he would **BARK, BARK, BARK**. He would bring his ball to his human, sit nicely, and wag his tail. Once he had his human's attention, he would **BARK, BARK, BARK**.

"BARK **BARK BARK**"

No matter what he did, Baxter could not get his human outside like before. Feeling sad, the little long dog got comfortable in his special spot and closed his eyes. With each breath in and out, his sadness began to float away on clouds of sweet memories in his little long dreams.

LISTEN LISTEN LISTEN

After a little rest, the little long dog opened his eyes and stretched a big stretch. After his stretch and a big shake, an idea came to Baxter. Sometimes, when he wanted his human to play, he would use the same trick as when he wanted delicious bites of food from his human's plate. Instead of saying **BARK, BARK, BARK**, he would sit quietly and *LISTEN, LISTEN, LISTEN*. When he would *LISTEN*, he would find clues to understand his human a little more.

LISTEN LISTEN LISTEN

Sure enough, when his **BARK, BARK, BARK** softened and turned into *LISTEN, LISTEN, LISTEN,* the little long dog noticed some clues. There were fewer smells in his home. Some of his favourite things could not be found. The blanket and pillow were both gone from his special spot. The familiar smells from the kitchen were replaced by the ring of the doorbell and scrumptious boxes and paper bags that his human would not share. Humans that Baxter had grown to know did not come to play anymore.

One July morning, the little long dog slowly opened his eyes to the morning sun on his face. To his surprise, his human was nowhere to be found! Confused, Baxter jumped down from his sleeping spot and moved through the now empty house in search of his human. This was a time for **BARK, BARK, BARK** not *LISTEN, LISTEN, LISTEN.* He saw his human with a smile on her face, a suitcase at her side, and the best thing of all...a little black bag. This was no ordinary little black bag and Baxter's tail began to wag. The bag was a sign that the little long dog was going on a great adventure.

"BARK **BARK BARK**"

The little long dog jumped into his black bag. This little black bag took Baxter and his human on many journeys. Sometimes Baxter would travel along the road, sometimes in the air, and sometimes, when he did not feel like moving his little legs, he would scurry into his exploration machine and have his human carry him. The car was his favourite. He loved to feel his ears flap in the wind and smell all the smells from the window. It was his lucky day! Sure enough, his human placed his bag in the car and off they went—just the little long dog and his human. Baxter began to **BARK, BARK, BARK** in delight!

After a little nap for the little long dog, Baxter slowly opened his eyes and stretched a long stretch. The window was open and the smells coming into the car were different and made him curious about what was outside the window. Rather than **BARK, BARK, BARK,** he did what little long dogs do best—he stretched and closed his eyes for another nap.

When he woke up, the little long dog started to feel scared. Whenever he would feel scared, he would **BARK, BARK, BARK.** His human sat in the front seat with her eyes focused on the window ahead. He felt frustrated. Why couldn't his human go back to the way they used to be? In this moment, when his human did not turn her head at **BARK, BARK, BARK,** he remembered something. He remembered that when he decided to *LISTEN, LISTEN, LISTEN,* he started his great adventure with his human. Maybe if the little long dog could *LISTEN, LISTEN, LISTEN,* he could help his human and try another way to be there for his special person.

Finally, the car came to a stop. The little long dog and his human got out of the car. His human tugged gently on Baxter's leash. Normally, this would signal him to move his little legs. This time, he stopped in his tracks. In front of him were big buildings **EVERYWHERE!** The familiar northern sky was nowhere to be found. He went **BARK, BARK** and then remembered before his last **BARK** that he would *LISTEN*.

Carefully, he followed his human through a door and onto a slippery floor. His human touched the wall, and all of a sudden Baxter heard a **BING** and then the silver wall in front began to open. He stopped and did not move when his human gently pulled the leash. In his spot on the slippery floor, he chose to not move with his human but to *LISTEN, LISTEN, LISTEN.*

As the silver wall opened farther, a small fluffy dog emerged with their human. The little long dog could not believe his eyes. Humans and dogs coming out of walls!

He took a step toward the small fluffy dog. Their noses touched, their tails wagged, and their humans smiled. Now Baxter was ready to walk towards whatever was on the other side of the silver wall. With his new trick and his human at his side, the little long dog could do anything!

The little long dog had spent his entire life with his human, in his special spot, and with the smells in his home. This place was different. He felt excitement and butterflies in his tummy. Usually when he felt this way, he would look at his human and **BARK, BARK, BARK.** This time, though, he stopped and started to *LISTEN, LISTEN,* and...*THINK!*

Once the little long dog had walked into the silver wall, his nose touched the ground and went crazy sniffing everywhere to follow the smells! Behind the silver wall was a shiny secret room. When Baxter looked up, he could see his human staring back at him. His nose told him that many dogs had been in this space. This secret room was another sign that the little long dog was on a great adventure.

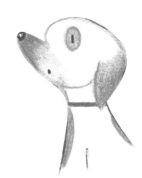

The little long dog went **BARK, BARK, BARK** as his human threw his ball. He was at his favourite place in his new home—a big open space with many dog friends, lots of different balls to chase, and a lingering salty smell. Whenever he went to this space with his human, if he could *LISTEN, LISTEN, LISTEN,* his human would get him a special treat. This special treat was cold on Baxter's tongue, and if he didn't lick it fast enough, it would disappear into a pool of liquid. The interesting thing about this special treat was that it was always yummy! When he would *THINK, THINK, THINK,* he would be ready for any great adventure with his human. Lately, his human smiled more, played more, and brought more special humans into the life of the little long dog.

As the Baxter continued to *THINK, THINK, THINK,* things that were scary to the little long dog at first didn't seem as bad now. He learned that a balcony was a place where people could be high in the sky and still get fresh air. This became one of his new special spots. He would roll on his back and warm his tummy on sunny days. On days where water fell from the sky, Baxter preferred sitting on the couch—it was the same comfy couch as before, but in a new house.

The little long dog learned many things from his adventure. The most important lesson was to *THINK, THINK, THINK.* Thinking helped him appreciate the gifts around him. He didn't even mind days when the cold pavement would touch his little long belly on his walks with his human. Today was a beautiful day. Baxter and his human walked out towards the magical blue waters and swimming sea critters. They looked at each other and smiled.

Author Jennifer Harrison is an educator who has worked in schools throughout British Columbia. Storytelling has been instrumental in Jennifer's life. Her most significant learning has come from the practice of sharing and listening to stories. She is the proud human to her trusted little long dog Baxter. This is her first piece of writing and is based on her journey with Baxter from Fort St. John to Vancouver.

Illustrator Harjoyt Johal is an educator in British Columbia. As a child, Harjoyt was inspired to doodle and create images through the endless picture books she read and cartoons she watched. This is Harjoyt's first illustration for a children's book. She was inspired to draw Baxter after forming a friendship with him and his human, Jennifer. Harjoyt hopes her experience will inspire other doodlers and drawers out there to pursue their creative habits.

The Adventure of the Little Long Dog is a collaboration between two British Columbia-based female educators and friends. The story is inspired by Jennifer's dachshund, Baxter, who is known for his spunky personality and loud bark. The intention of sharing Baxter's story is a way to promote understanding from multiple perspectives and support the teaching of empathy.

The story also provided an opportunity to showcase the vastness and beauty of British Columbia. Baxter's journey is based on Jennifer's re-location from Fort St. John, located in the Peace River Region to Vancouver, in the Lower Mainland. This was an impactful transition, and while it was challenging, it opened up opportunities and lifelong friendships for both Jennifer and Baxter.

Printed in the USA
CPSIA information can be obtained
at www.ICGtesting.com
LVHW060358210224
772425LV00022B/150